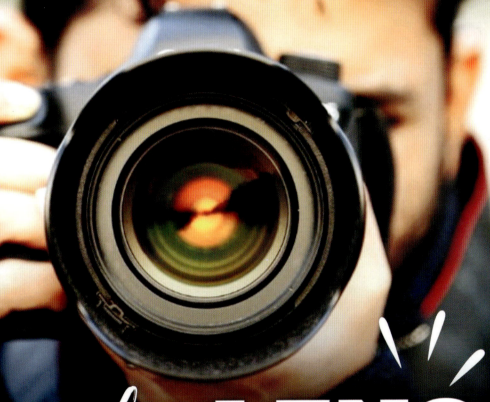

Copyright © 2023 by Storyshares. All rights reserved.

Black Rabbit Tales is an imprint of
Black Rabbit Books
P.O. Box 227
Mankato, MN 56001
www.blackrabbitbooks.com

This library-bound edition is published in 2025 by
Black Rabbit Books, by arrangement with:

Storyshares, LLC
24 N. Bryn Mawr Avenue #340
Bryn Mawr, PA 19010-3304
www.storyshares.org

Printed in China.

The characters and events in this book are fictitious. Any similarity to real persons, living or dead, is entirely coincidental.

Library of Congress Cataloging-in-Publication Data
Names: Agbangbatin, Pius, author. | Quinton, James, author. Title: With a pen and a lens / Pius Agbangbatin, James Quinton. Description: Library edition. | Mankato, MN: Black Rabbit Tales, 2025. | Series: These first letters | Focuses on consonant digraphs. | Audience: Ages 10–14. | Audience: Grades 4–6. | Summary: "Carlos and Whit live in very different places, but they both use their photos and words to share the beauty of their homes with the world"—Provided by publisher.
Identifiers: LCCN 2024023229 | ISBN 9781644668948 (library binding) Subjects: LCSH: Readers (Primary) | English language—Consonants—Juvenile literature. | Photography—Juvenile literature. | Reading—Phonetic method—Juvenile literature. | LCGFT: Readers (Publications). Classification: LCC PE1119.2 .A34 2025 | DDC 428.6/2—dc23/eng/20240620
LC record available at https://lccn.loc.gov/202402322

**Aligned with the Science of Reading.
Interest Level: 4th grade and beyond.**

WITH A PEN AND A LENS

PIUS AGBANGBATIN
JAMES QUINTON

A DECODABLES CHAPTER BOOK

TABLE OF CONTENTS

JAMES QUINTON	A DAY AT THE RIVER	1
PIUS AGBANGBATIN	WHALE OF A DAY	16
JAMES QUINTON	FRIENDS OF THE FOREST	28
JAMES QUINTON	TEEN JAZZ	38

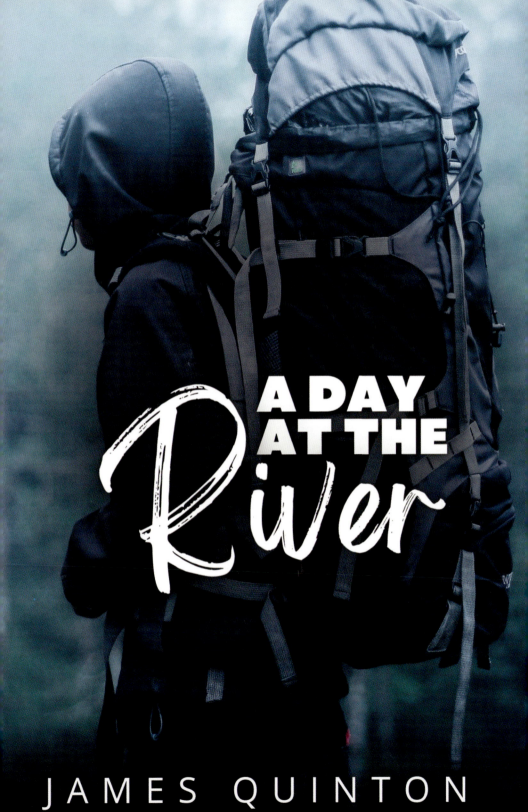

A DAY AT THE RIVER

JAMES QUINTON

| Phonics Guide

"A Day at the River"

consonant digraphs: ch, ph, kn

ch
- chirped
- check
- lunch
- watched
- chipmunks
- choose
- such
- much

ph
- phone
- photos
- dolphin
- photographer

kn
- knees
- knapsack
- knew
- know
- knot
- knelt

high frequency words

- was
- had
- looked
- that
- been
- with
- people
- years
- more
- make
- there

challenge words

- camera
- rainforest
- popular
- otters

1

1

Birds sang.

Frogs chirped.

The sun was not yet up.

But Carlos was.

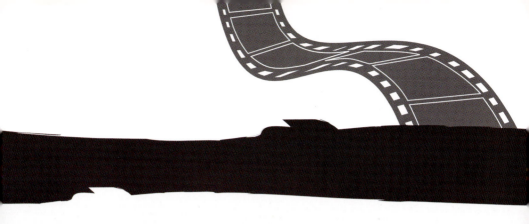

He was on his knees, packing his knapsack.

Camera? *Check.*

Pad? *Check.*

Lunch? *Check.*

Water? *Check.*

He looked down at his phone.

It was open to his Pic-Share page.

He had been snapping photos for a long time.

They were of the rainforest he knew to be his home.

A pal told him one day that he should be on Pic-Share.

That way, lots of people would know about his photos.

His page was now five years old. And very popular.

He saw that his post from last night had hundreds of likes.

The photo was an empty box with just two words.

Pink. Dolphin.

He knew that would make his fans happy!

They had been asking him for weeks to look for that animal.

Today, he was going to do just that.

He tied a knot at the top of his bag.

Then he tucked his phone into his pants.

Time to go.

It took a bit of time for him to get to the Napo River.

He had to check his map a lot.

At last, he knelt by the water and set up his camera.

He knew there was just one more thing to do. *Wait.*

He watched the waters.

He saw otters. He saw fish. He saw a lot of birds.

He saw chipmunks. And rabbits. And even a deer.

But no dolphin.

It was getting late.

And Carlos was getting upset.

Did he choose a bad day?

Did he choose a bad spot?

No, he did not.

At last, there it was.

Carlos had never seen such a pretty animal.

It looked at him while his camera snapped photos.

It even gave him a nod.

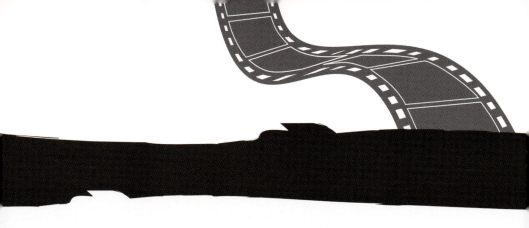

"Did you know I was trying to find you?" he asked.

The dolphin jumped.

"You did!" Carlos said. "You're such a smart animal."

He was sad when the dolphin left.

But he also knew that he was very, very lucky.

"Thank you," he said to the water. Then he packed his knapsack just like before.

"Thank you so much."

CarlosInTheWoods   •••

1,530	51.2K	2,236
Posts	Followers	Following

Carlos
Photographer | Animal Pal

I love the forest. I love animals. And I love to snap photos of them. Get to know me!

 Followed by **Destiny** and **Sara**

PINK DOLPHIN

WHALE OF A DAY

PIUS AGBANGBATIN

Phonics Guide

"Whale of a Day"

**consonant digraphs: wh, wr, ck
welded sounds ending with -ng**

digraph: wh

Whit
whizzed
whale
Whoopie

where
whirl
while

digraph: wr

write
wrong
wrote

digraph: ck

checked   thick
quickly   sack
picked   back
checked   Beck
black   truck

lumberjack
backpack
snack
checker
knapsack
dock
tickets

lucky
humpback
rucksack
crackers
duck

-ng welded sounds

wing
waiting
watching
bring

wrong
swung
hungry

high frequency words

of
he
with
where
were

there
asked
soon

challenge words

showered
clothes
wondered
smooth
favorite

16

2

Whit's watch whizzed. He checked the time. It was 9 am.

He showered quickly and picked out his clothes.

He went with a checked shirt and black pants.

Then he lifted a thick sack onto his back. He heard Beck's truck.

Beck was a lumberjack, and Whit's pal. He picked Whit up to take him to work most days.

Whit worked on a whale watch in Benin, Africa.

His ship was called Write Wing. There was a part of the ship called a wing where Whit would write. It was his job to take notes about the whales he saw.

Whoopie was waiting at the whale watch. She was watching the waves when Whit got there.

She had wondered where Whit was.

In her backpack was a snack for her. She had also packed a snack for Whit.

"Whit, where were you?" Whoopie asked. She hopped up and down.

Whoopie was a checker for Write Wing. It was her job to give out tickets on land.

But today Whit got to bring Whoopie with him onto the water.

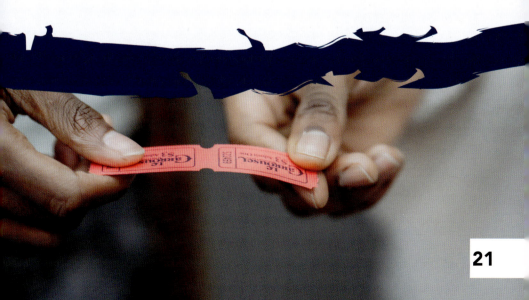

"We took a wrong turn," Whit said. He swung his knapsack onto his back. "Let's go!"

Whit and Whoopie ran to the whale watching ship.

Soon it would leave the dock.

Whit and Whoopie were lucky to make it. It was such a good day to go out on the ship!

The waters were smooth. The sun was warm.

Whit and Whoopie watched the whales whirl in the water.

Whit made notes while he watched. He wrote about how many whales they saw. And what kind.

There were killer whales.

And humpback whales.

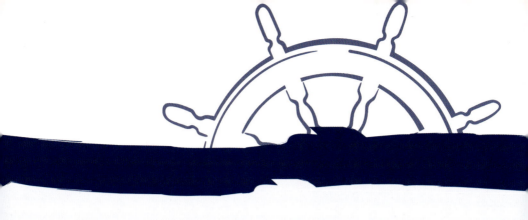

On the way back to the dock, Whit got hungry.

Whoopie checked her rucksack.

She took out some crackers. She gave them to Whit.

"Wow, thanks!" Whit said.

When they got to the dock, Whoopie yelled. "I want to go back!" she said.

Whit knew how she felt. It was always like that for him when the ship got back to the dock.

"We will," he said.

Date: August 12   Location: Benin

Notes:

Today we got to spot 7 whales. The Write Wing left the dock at 10 am. The waters were very flat. It was not hard to spot the first whale. It was a humpback. Her name is Ducky. I know because she put her tail up for us. There's a spot on her back that looks like a duck. She is one of my favorite whales.

Friends of the Forest

JAMES QUINTON

FRIENDS OF THE FOREST

JAMES QUINTON

 | Phonics Guide

"Friends of the Forest"

consonant digraphs: sh, th
consonant trigraphs: tch, dge

digraph: sh
- slash
- brush
- cash
- share

digraph: th
- there
- this
- the
- other
- their
- they
- with
- them
- then
- without

trigraph: tch
- batch
- watch
- clutched

trigraph: dge
- badges
- pledged
- pledge

high frequency words

- asked
- friends
- used
- down
- would
- food
- other
- numbers
- their
- could
- love
- was
- wanted
- would
- them
- over

challenge words

- protest
- losing
- profits
- ranches
- cattle
- videos
- exist

28

NO MORE SLASH AND BURN.

Carlos used a brush to make the big, red letters.

F.O.T.F. had asked for his help.

F.O.T.F. stood for Friends of the Forest.

They were having a big protest.

There were farms that wanted to burn a big batch of the forest down.

This would be very bad and so, so sad.

The forest where Carlos lived is one of a kind.

More birds lived there than in any other spot in the world.

It had the most animals who were at risk, too.

At risk means their numbers were getting very small.

They were losing their homes and their food.

The forest where Carlos lived was one of the last spots where they could live too.

The farms wanted to burn the forest so that they could make profits.

They wanted to grow corn to sell. They wanted to set up ranches for cattle.

Burning the forest was a fast way to get the land they needed to make cash.

Carlos would not let this happen. He would not watch his forest burn.

He went with the F.O.T.F. to protest.

He had badges he made for them to put on their jackets.

And posters he made for them to hold.

Then Carlos clutched his camera.

And he did what he did best.

He took photos.

So many photos. And videos for his fans to watch.

He pledged to share all that he saw.

With his pictures, he shared facts.

This forest is the lungs of our world.

It gives us our air.

It is home to half of the plants and animals in the world.

Lots of them can't exist without it.

Last of all, he shared a pledge.

The pledge asked fans to help save the forest.

With the pledge, he shared one more fact.

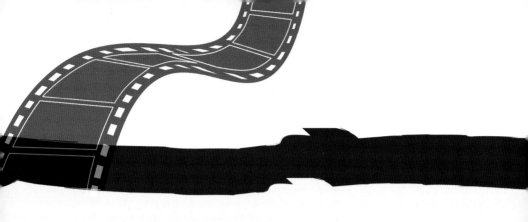

This fact made him the most sad.

But it also gave him the most hope.

The next day, over 40,000 fans had put their names on the pledge.

Maybe it was not too late.

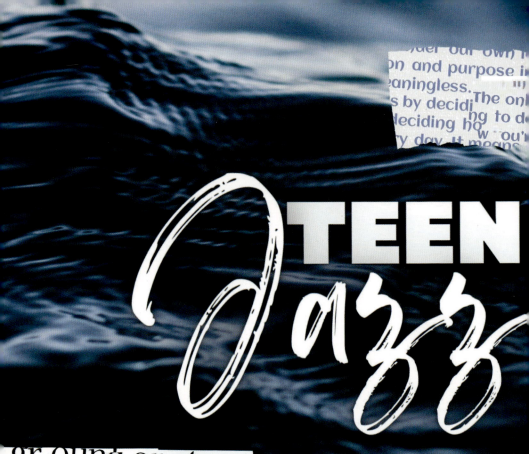

TEEN Jazz

JAMES QUINTON

TEEN JAZZ

JAMES QUINTON

 | Phonics Guide

"Teen Jazz"

bonus letters: ff, ll, ss, zz

letter sound: ff

waffle
baffled

letter sound: ll

Della   fall*
called*   all*
tall*   yelled
pulled   still
yell

*Words that can also be used to practice the welded letters "all."

letter sound: ss

across
passed

letter sound: zz

jazz
jazzed
Lizz

high frequency words

waiting   out   Ecuador
mother   with
time   world
over   were
pulled   come

challenge words

nervous   science
envelope   magazine
copy   whale
           talent

38

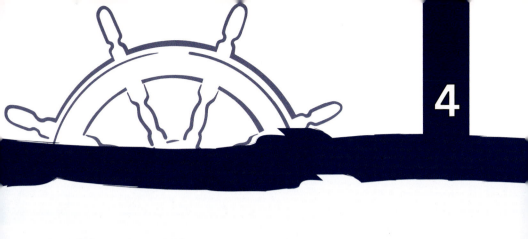

4

Whit's ship, the Write Wing, had just made it back to the dock.

His mom, Della, was waiting for him. That made Whit nervous.

His mom worked at the Waffle House this time of day.

"Whit!" she called. He ran over to her.

She was holding a tall folder.

"Is everything okay?" Whit asked.

His mom smiled. "Better than okay," she said. She handed him the envelope. "Open it."

Whit pulled out a copy of "Teen Jazz."

It was a science magazine with readers all across the world.

"Cool!" Whit said.

His mom shook her head. "No, no. Look in it!" she said. She was so happy that her voice was more of a yell.

Whit passed over the first few pages. Then he stopped.

"No way," he said. He felt like he might fall over. "Mom!"

"I know!" she said. "I'm so jazzed, Whit! You did it!"

Whit looked at the page again.

He had sent his whale watching notes to Teen Jazz back in the fall.

Now... here they were! In the best teen magazine, if you asked Whit!

He was baffled.

the dock at 10 am. The waters were very flat. It was not hard to spot the first whale. It was a humpback. Her name is Ducky. I know because she put her tail up for us. There's a spot on her back that looks like a duck. She is one of my favorite whales.

"I called the Waffle House," his mom said. "They got Lizz to take my shift. We're gonna go party. Your pal Whoopie can come too!"

Whit didn't know what to say. It was all hitting him at once.

He kept turning the pages of the magazine.

There was so much talent inside.

Teens doing important work all over the world.

He read about a girl named Destiny in the Bahamas.

She was getting crews to pick up trash from beaches around the world.

He read about a boy named Carlos in Ecuador.

He was using his photos to save the rainforest that was his home.

Whit felt proud to have his story shared beside theirs.

"No way!" a girl yelled.

Whit turned to see Whoopie running at him.

"I am not the only one who is jazzed," Whit's mom said.

She winked at Whit. "You ready to go?" she asked.

Whit nodded. He was still too happy for words.

"This is the best day," he said.

Date: August 18   Location: Benin

Notes:

Today I spotted an African manatee, which is a rare thing to see here! Here are some facts that I looked up about it:

It is gray, but can look green or brown. This is because of the plants that grow on it.

They do not just live in the ocean. They also live in lakes and rivers!

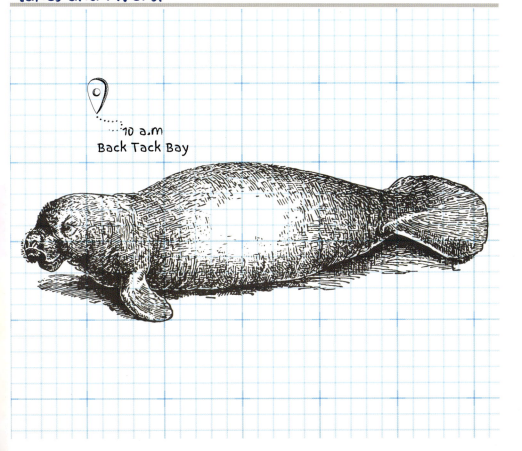

10 a.m
Back Tack Bay

About the Authors

Pius Agbangbatin is one of the winners of the Storyshares 2021 Story of the Year Contest. Pius is from Benin, West Africa, and wrote the book *Born in Danger.*

Pius' experience as a writer started almost eight years ago. He's always been an avid reader, and he developed his passion for writing in senior secondary school. Now, he has decided to turn his passion into a career.

James Quinton is a writer from a small town in central Massachusetts. When he's not at his desk, he's either in his garden coaxing his plants to grow or in his workshop turning salvaged wood and flea market finds into one-of-a-kind furniture and home decor.

About The Publisher

Storyshares is a nonprofit focused on supporting the millions of teens and adults who struggle with reading by creating a new shelf in the library specifically for them. The ever-growing collection features content that is compelling and culturally relevant for teens and adults, yet still readable at a range of lower reading levels.

Storyshares generates content by engaging deeply with writers, bringing together a community to create this new kind of book. With more intriguing and approachable stories to choose from, the teens and adults who have fallen behind are improving their skills and beginning to discover the joy of reading. For more information, visit storyshares.org.

Easy to Read. Hard to Put Down.